This
Treasure Cove Story
belongs to

_____

**SPIDER-MAN
HIGH VOLTAGE!**

A CENTUM BOOK 978-1-912396-74-0
Published in Great Britain by Centum Books Ltd.
This edition published 2018.

3 5 7 9 10 8 6 4 2

Centum Books Ltd, 20 Devon Square, Newton Abbot,
Devon, TQ12 2HR, UK.

www.centumbooksltd.co.uk | books@centumbooksltd.co.uk
CENTUM BOOKS Limited Reg. No. 07641486.

A CIP catalogue record for this book is available
from the British Library.

Printed in China.

A Treasure Cove Story

MARVEL
SPIDER-MAN™

High Voltage!

Based on the stories by Marvel Comics
By Frank Berrios
Illustrated by Francesco Legramandi
and Andrea Cagol

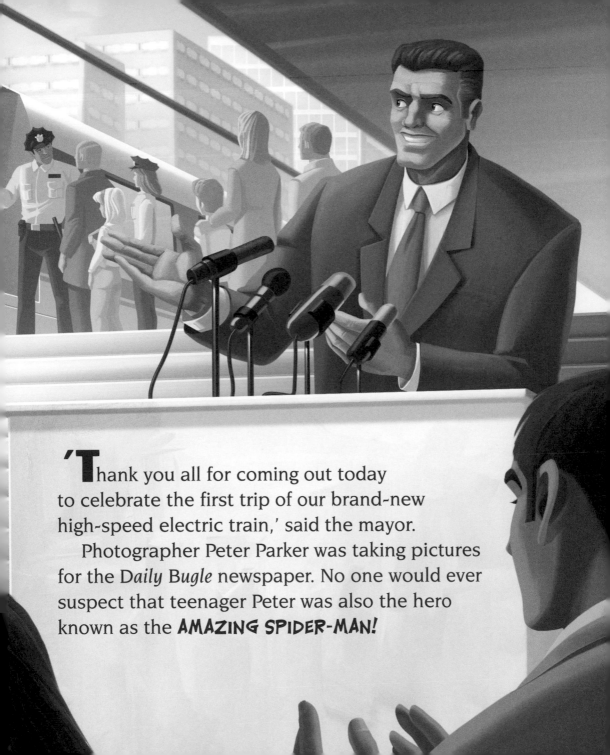

'**T**hank you all for coming out today to celebrate the first trip of our brand-new high-speed electric train,' said the mayor.

Photographer Peter Parker was taking pictures for the *Daily Bugle* newspaper. No one would ever suspect that teenager Peter was also the hero known as the **AMAZING SPIDER-MAN!**

As Peter made his way through the crowd, his **spider-sense** suddenly started to tingle – there was danger nearby!

'Sorry to SHOCK you,' the villain Electro said, zapping a guard with a bolt of electricity. 'But I have a little banking to do downtown and this electric train will be the perfect getaway vehicle for my withdrawal!'

Peter raced off to find a place to make
a quick change into his Spider-Man costume.
Meanwhile, Electro released a surge of power,
causing the lights and cameras to **explode!**

'All aboard the Electro Express!' announced the villain.

With a powerful SPARK from his hands, Electro started the electric train to make his escape. Little did he know, Spider-Man was in pursuit!

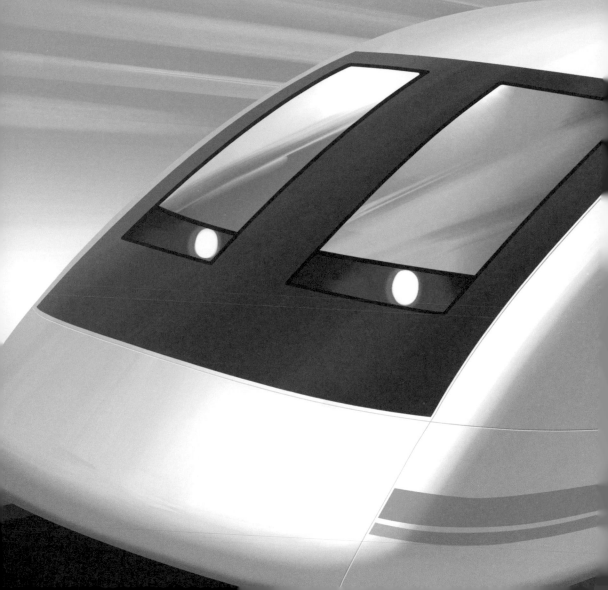

'I hope you weren't going to leave without saying goodbye to your friendly neighbourhood Spider-Man!' joked the **web-slinger**. With a mighty kick, he sent Electro flying!

'Spider-Man!' yelled Electro. 'I'll zap you like the bug you are!'

Electro threw a bolt of electricity that destroyed the control panel, slowing the train.

'Guess this is my stop!' said Spider-Man. The web-slinger dashed deeper into the dark train tunnel. He wanted to make sure no one was around to get hurt by the **super-charged** bad guy.

'There's nowhere to run!' Electro yelled,
unleashing his power on Spider-Man.

Electro hit Spider-Man with a burst of electricity. 'Now let's see if lightning can strike twice,' he snarled, getting ready to zap the wall-crawler again.

'I need a plan,' Spidey thought as he struggled to stay on his feet.

'I think it's time for **lights-out** and
a nap!' Spidey joked. Using his web-shooters,
Spider-Man covered Electro's eyes with webbing
so thick that the villain couldn't see!

'This web of yours won't stop me for long!'
the villain growled. 'My electric powers can
burn through anything!'

The angry villain chased Spider-Man out
of the tunnel and into a darkened building.

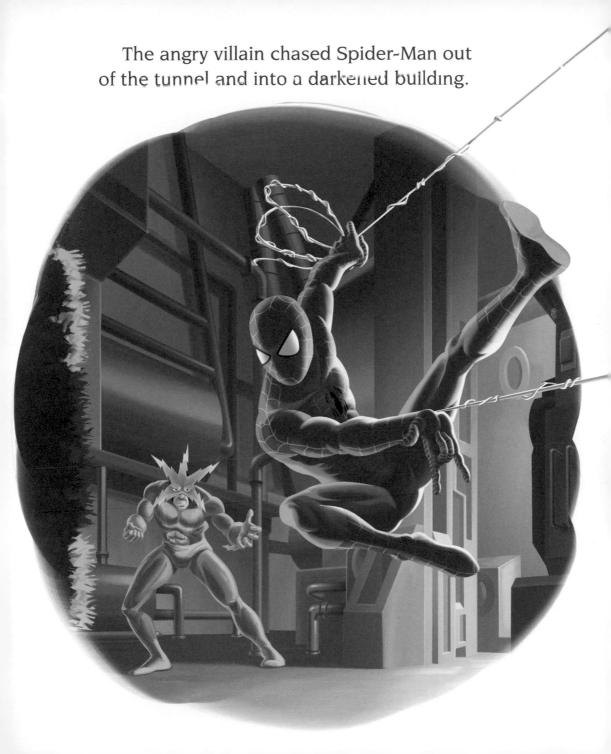

'I think it's time for you to cool off!' said Spider-Man. With the pull of a lever, lights turned on and machines whirred to life.

'**Nooo!**' screamed Electro. Two huge spinning car-wash brushes popped out and spun Electro around like a top. Then two spray nozzles covered him with soap and water!

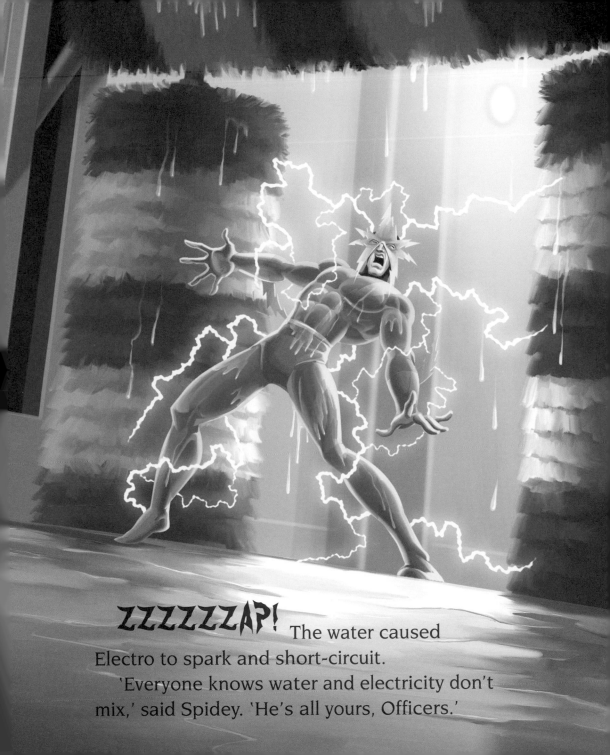

ZZZZZZAP! The water caused
Electro to spark and short-circuit.
'Everyone knows water and electricity don't
mix,' said Spidey. 'He's all yours, Officers.'

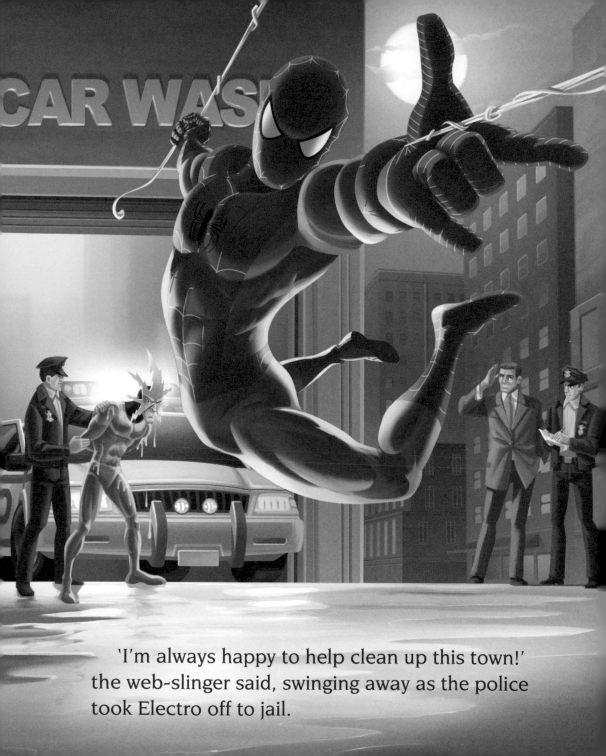

'I'm always happy to help clean up this town!' the web-slinger said, swinging away as the police took Electro off to jail.

 # Treasure Cove Stories

Book list may be subject to change.